Babyfather

by

Joanna Kenrick

Illustrated by Julia Page

Published in 2007 in Great Britain by
Barrington Stoke Ltd
18 Walker Street, Edinburgh EH3 7LP

www.barringtonstoke.co.uk

ISBN: 978-1-84299-469-6

Printed in Great Britain by Bell & Bain Ltd

A Note from the Author

There are lots of books about teenage pregnancy out there. Some of them are really good. But most of them tell the girl's story – after all, it's her body, isn't it? Her baby.

But it takes two to make a baby. Two to make a mistake. And I wondered – how does it feel to be the boy here? Everyone fusses over the girl. Everyone cares about the girl. The boy is left out in the cold. How does that feel?

For all the Mickeys out there

Contents

1   Can We Talk?   1

2   Bad News Travels Fast   13

3   Aunt Kelly Talks Sense   27

4   Facing Up   40

Chapter 1
Can We Talk?

We didn't mean it to happen. Everyone says that, don't they? I never thought Emma would get pregnant. She's sure to be on the Pill, I thought.

No, I didn't. That's a lie. I didn't think about it at all. We just did it.

And then she phoned me. "That you, Mickey?" Her voice sounded all wobbly.

"Hi. You OK?"

"No, I'm not. Can we talk?"

My heart sank. I hate it when girls say "Can we talk?" Most of the time this means "I'm not happy about the way you're treating me." Most of the time, I don't get a word in. They moan about how I don't ring them every hour of every day. Or how

I haven't said "I love you" for a week. Or how I never buy them presents.

So I wasn't looking forward to the "talk". But it was even more awful than I'd thought.

"I don't know how to say this," she said when we met. "So I'm just going to come out with it."

"OK." Was she dumping me?

"I'm pregnant."

I laughed. I thought she was joking. "No way!"

Her face crumpled and she started crying. Then I knew she wasn't joking.

"God." Well, OK, that's not *quite* the word I used. "How come?"

She looked at me like I was mad. "How do you think? Don't you go to biology lessons with the rest of us?"

I blushed. "Yeah, of course. But, I mean – wasn't that your first time?"

"What's that got to do with it?"

"I didn't think you could get pregnant the first time," I said.

"Well, you were wrong."

"Why aren't you on the Pill?"

"Why didn't you use a condom?" She was angry now. "Don't try to blame me for this."

"I wasn't!" I said.

"This is your mistake too."

I didn't know what to say. "What are you going to do?"

"What do you mean?" She gave me an angry look. "Are you saying I should get rid of it?"

"Well, yes. If you don't want it."

"If *I* don't want it? Oh, thanks, so I get to decide all on my own, do I?" Her voice was getting higher and higher.

I was starting to get cross. "What's it got to do with me? You're the one who's pregnant."

"Yeah, and you're the one who got me in this state!" Tears were running down her cheeks. I hate it when girls cry – it makes me jumpy. "I'm only 15, Mickey, what am I going to do?"

"How would I know? I'm only three months older than you."

She started really crying then – big, choking sobs. I tried to put my arms around her. She pushed me away.

"Don't. I don't want you to touch me right now. I can't think. I'll call you." She picked up her bag and left.

I felt really bad. I mean *really* bad. I could see I'd been a bit stupid. Not thinking she could get pregnant, that is. But I felt angry too. If she knew she could get pregnant the first time, why didn't she say? I don't remember her asking me to

put on a condom when we went to bed. Not
that I had any condoms anyway. I thought
condoms were to stop you getting AIDS.

And now she was pregnant.

I was going to be a dad.

Chapter 2
Bad News Travels Fast

I didn't tell my parents. I didn't know how to. But my mate Josh found out at school.

"Is it true you got Emma up the duff?"

How had he found out so fast? "Who told you?" I asked.

"Emma told Cathy, who told Pari, who told Olly, who told me."

"God."

"So it's true then?"

"Yeah, I guess. Well, she wouldn't lie, would she?"

Josh looked around and then came a bit closer. "Are you sure it's yours, mate?"

I looked at him, puzzled. "What do you mean?"

"Well, you know what girls are like. How do you know it's yours?"

"Are you saying she's a slag?"

"No, mate, course not." Josh gave a shrug. "Don't stress. I was just saying you can't trust them sometimes."

"Well, I trust Emma," I said. "Besides, she was a virgin before me."

"So she says," muttered Josh.

"Now, you shut up," I said angrily. "You don't know what you're talking about."

"OK, OK. Whatever you say. So what's she going to do about it?"

"That's what I asked. But she got all narky with me. Said she couldn't decide on her own. She kept asking *me* what she should do."

Josh looked puzzled. "But she's the one who's pregnant, not you."

That made me feel better. "See, that's what I said! But then she just started crying."

Josh shook his head. "Girls. Useless."

But the rest of the girls at school didn't act useless. They were all out to get me.

"You git," hissed Sophie in English.

"How could you be so stupid?" muttered Cathy in Geography.

"I hope you're going to do the right thing," said Nicole in Maths.

"The right thing?" I was puzzled. "What right thing?"

Nicole said nothing, but just raised her eye-brows at me.

I had an awful thought. Did she mean I should ask Emma to marry me? Dear God, no! I wasn't ready to get married. Not now – not for years and years. Besides, I didn't love Emma. Hold on, that makes me sound really mean. I did like Emma a lot. I went to bed with her, didn't I? But love her so much I wanted to marry her? I don't think so!

School was really bad. By morning break every single person knew – even the teachers, I reckon.

I was made to go and see the school counsellor. She was a stupid-looking woman called Miss Dobson, with big glasses and wispy hair.

"Michael, I want to talk about this whole thing with you and Emma," said Dobby.

"Fine. Talk all you want," I said in a polite voice.

She looked cross. "You do understand that this is important, don't you?"

I felt angry. "Of course I do. She's going to have a baby. She'll have to leave school. No uni, blah, blah. Important. I get it."

"I don't think you understand," said Dobby. "This is important for you too."

"Why?"

"Because the two of you are in this together. You're going to be a father."

This was still such a weird idea that I laughed.

Dobby made a tutting noise. "It's not funny, Michael. You're going to have to grow up very fast."

"I am grown up."

"Well, you're not behaving that way."

Oh, here we go. The old "I don't like your attitude" speech. I didn't bother to listen for the next ten minutes. In the end she gave up. "I really think you need to talk to Emma," she said.

"I did that. She doesn't want to talk to me any more."

"Yes, well, that doesn't surprise me," said Dobby. "You've only got yourself to blame."

I was shocked. I thought school counsellors were there to help you!

Chapter 3
Aunt Kelly Talks Sense

My day got even worse when I got home. Emma's mum had phoned my mum and she was practically foaming at the mouth.

"How could you be such a prat? After all those sex lessons in biology too!"

I didn't tell her that I spent most of our sex ed lessons sniggering at the back with Josh.

"I feel so let down! What if Emma asks for money for the baby? We don't have much money as it is, living on my wages." And on and on. "I've had to tell your Aunt Kelly. She was coming for dinner anyway. Maybe she can talk some sense into you, but I guess it's too late now."

I was quite pleased that Aunt Kelly was coming. She's sensible and doesn't yell at me. But I felt kind of bad that she knew about the baby. I respected her. I didn't want her to think I was a prat.

Aunt Kelly gave me a big hug and said, "Well, you've got yourself into a bit of a mess, haven't you?"

And suddenly I felt like I was going to cry. She was the only one who hadn't had a go at me. But I couldn't cry, of course. That would be wussy. So I just laughed and said, "Yeah, looks like it."

After dinner, Aunt Kelly and I sat on the sofa. Mum was in the kitchen, washing up. Most times she gets me to do it.

"So, how's it going?" asked Aunt Kelly. "How are you coping?"

I shrugged. "Dunno. Everyone keeps yelling at me, but I don't really see why. I wasn't to know."

Aunt Kelly raised an eye-brow.

"Well, OK. Maybe I made a mistake. But what's the point in yelling at me now? I can't do anything about it."

Aunt Kelly nodded. "I agree. There's no point shutting the barn door once the horse has got out."

"Huh?"

"What you said. There's no point telling you off now – it's too late." She sat back. "Is Emma going to keep the baby?"

"I don't know. She started talking about it and then she kept crying. I couldn't get any sense out of her."

"She's scared," said Aunt Kelly. "Really scared."

I shrugged. "Yeah, I guess."

"Being pregnant is a big thing for a girl. You grow another person inside of you. How scary would that be?"

I thought about the film *Alien* where this metal monster thing explodes out of people. "Very scary," I agreed.

"Plus, when the baby comes, she's got to look after it all the time. You two aren't married and I don't suppose you will be."

"No way!"

"Then she's going to have to do all the looking after. She'll wake up every single night for at least the first few months. She won't sleep for more than three hours at a time. She'll be tired all the time. The baby will cry and shit, because that's what babies do. And worst of all, she'll know she can't ever be free again."

I looked at Aunt Kelly. "I thought girls liked babies. You sound as if you hate them."

She laughed. "I don't hate them. And yes, girls like babies, but no-one understands how much work it is until you've got one. There are nice moments, but your life isn't your own any more. She

will never be just 'Emma' again. She'll be 'Emma with a baby'. And while her friends are all out clubbing and drinking, she'll be stuck at home with her child. Being sensible."

I gulped. It sounded horrendous. "Well, what can I do? I said. "I don't want a baby either."

"I know you don't. And guess what – you're the lucky one. You get to hand it back to her when you're sick of it."

"Hand it back? After doing what?"

Aunt Kelly looked me in the eye. "After spending some time with your son or daughter. To give Emma a break. You're going to support her and be there when she needs a helping hand."

"Am I?"

She didn't blink. "Yes. You are."

So I went round to Emma's house.

Chapter 4
Facing Up

Her mum didn't want to let me in.
"Don't you think you've done enough?" she
hissed at me.

"Please," I said. "I need to see her.

In the end she let me in. "Emma's in the sitting room."

Emma was sitting on the sofa, staring at the floor. I was shocked by how pale she was. She must have been crying for hours. She looked up. "What are you doing here?"

I knew Emma's mum was standing behind me. "I came to see you." I sounded pathetic. "Can we talk?"

She smiled a bit. "I thought you hated having a talk."

"Yeah, well, things are different now."

Emma's mum gave a snort. "They are indeed."

Emma got up. "Let's go in the garden." She shot a look at her mum as we went out. Her mum didn't come out after us.

The garden was a bit over-grown but there was a bench by a flower bed and we sat down. It wasn't that warm, but at least we were out of the house.

There was silence. Then it dawned on me that Emma was expecting me to start "the talk".

"I'm really sorry," I said. "I've been – a bit of a prat."

She smiled at that. "Looks like we both have."

"Anyway," I said. "I was talking to my aunt and she made me see some things."

"Like what?"

"Like how life is going to be different. For you. In a big way. And how I should do something to help."

Emma turned to face me. "Help how?"

"Well, I've been thinking about it. It's my baby too, so I should do some grown up stuff."

She laughed out loud. "Grown up stuff? Are you sure you're OK, Mickey? You never do any grown up stuff."

"Well, now I do. I'm going to be helpful. Look after the baby sometimes. Take it to the park. Teach it to play football."

"What if it's a girl?"

"She'll still learn football. I'm not sexist. And she'll support West Ham."

Emma laughed again, but then her face fell. "It's not all going to be fun, you know, Mickey."

"I know. There'll be crying and shit. And maybe she'll turn out to be crap at football. I know it won't all be easy."

"No."

I reached out for her hand. "But I'm going to help. To be here for you. Like family."

She squeezed my hand. "Are you going soft on me, Mickey Evans?"

I snatched my hand away. "No way! I'm being a man, that's all. Men look after their women."

"Who says I'm your woman?" she said sharply.

"The baby does."

There was another silence.

"Don't get rid of it," I said suddenly. "I really mean that. Please don't. I'll be there."

She looked hard at me, as if she was trying to see right into my head. "I was never really going to get rid of it," she said. "I did think about it but I don't think I could." She reached for my hand again. "It scares me, Mickey. Things are going to be different."

"I know. I guess I'll have to get a job."

"What about school?"

I laughed. "More studying? Please! I was going to leave at the end of this year anyway. I'm not good with learning from books. But I'll make sure I do my exams. I'll still be around for you and the baby."

"You promise?"

"I promise. Besides," I said, "my mum and aunt are big on keeping promises. I'd never hear the end of it if I let you down."

Emma's face broke into a beaming smile. She looked really pretty. "I suddenly remember why I like you," she said, and gave me a hug.

I hugged her back. Inside, part of me was in a panic. But the rest of me felt really in control. *You can do this*, I thought. *You may not be very good at it, but you can do it. If she can bring up a child, you can too.*

And it won't be fun all the time. There'll be crying and shit. But there'll be good bits too. And maybe I could do with a bit of growing up. Not too much, mind.

Just a bit.

Barrington Stoke would like to thank all its readers for commenting on the manuscript before publication and in particular:

Anne Carr
Emma Rogers

Become a Consultant!

Would you like to give us feedback on our titles before they are published? Contact us at the address below – we'd love to hear from you!

Email: info@barringtonstoke.co.uk
Website: www.barringtonstoke.co.uk

More exciting titles ...

Stray

by

David Belbin

EVEN IN A GANG, SHE'S ON HER OWN.

Stray's in with the wrong lot.

Can Kev save her?

Or will she drag him down?

More exciting titles ...

Perfect
by
Joanna Kenrick

TOO GOOD TO BE TRUE?

Dan and Kate are perfect together.

Nothing can go wrong.

Until the lying starts ...

You can order *Perfect* directly from our website
at **www.barringtonstoke.co.uk**